# For Nina Royle

British Library Cataloguing in Publication Data
Garland, Sarah
Going Swimming
I. Title
823'.914 (J)
ISBN 0–370–31450–6

Copyright © Sarah Garland 1990
Main text set in 28pt Century Schoolbook by
Wyvern Typesetting Ltd, Bristol

Printed in Great Britain by
Eagle Colourbooks Ltd.

The Bodley Head Children's Books
20 Vauxhall Bridge Road, London SW1V 2SA

*First published 1990*
*Reprinted 1990*

# GOING SWIMMING

## Sarah Garland

### THE BODLEY HEAD
London

# Stay there, good dog.

# We're going swimming.

# Get undressed.

# Fold the clothes.

Here's the pool.

# Jump in!

# Come on baby.

# Look! It's fun!

# Hold on tight.

# Float and kick.

# We've got to go.

# A warm drink

# and home again.